THE RENEGADE

Disney

'TRON

UPRISING

THE RENEGADE

ADAPTED BY SCOTT BEATTY

BASED ON A TELEPLAY BY KAMRAN PASHA

ORIGINAL STORY BY EDWARD KITSIS & ADAM HOROWITZ & KAMRAN PASHA

Disney PRESS

NEW YORK

First Edition
1 3 5 7 9 10 8 6 4 2
V475-2873-0-12136
ISBN 978-1-4231-5417-4

Visit disney.go.com/xd/tron

CHAPTER 1

THE OUTLANDS WERE A BARREN WASTELAND, a dead ocean of simulated ice stretching endlessly to the cold, black horizon. There was the Grid—where life teemed—and then there was everything else, the lifeless Outlands. The edge of the digital world. A cold and dark place.

In the Outlands there was only the wind, which swept the landscape clean of random, unintegrated pixels, moaning low over the crystalline surface. Constant. Except for the rising hum of an engine, a Light Cycle racing across the ice. The Light Cycle trailed a ribbon of light behind it.

Beck crouched low on his Light Cycle to minimize the Outlands' perpetual chill. Navigating into a more treacherous patch, Beck steered the vehicle through the switchbacks of ice dunes. He throttled up and the Light Cycle climbed a massive dune, plunging over the peak. He landed on the other side in a puff of ice crystals as the Light Cycle's wheels spun for purchase. Then he rocketed forward again, his path traced behind him in a zigzag. The light ribbon would dissipate soon, but for now it was the only new structure—the only structure, period—that had altered the physical dimensions of the Outlands.

Beck smiled to himself as he zoomed on, intact. *Made it.*

However, Beck's smile vanished just as swiftly as another Light Cycle emerged from the darkness, racing toward him from the side. The rider was masked behind a dark helmet. In another few seconds they would be face-to-face, assuming one of them didn't freeze first.

Beck revved his engine and increased his speed, but the pursuer still gained. So Beck skipped a line—*go to plan B*—and swerved his Light Cycle back and forth in quick jerks, his light ribbon undulating in a helix pattern behind him. Then Beck made a hard right, a ninety-degree turn that would have blocked the mysterious rider's trajectory if the pursuer didn't execute his own parallel turn with graceful ease. Whoever he was, he was *good*. There was no shaking him.

Beck didn't have to glance back any longer. His pursuer had pulled alongside him now and was driving dangerously close. Navigating the ice was hard enough without worrying over a collision—

Beck was jolted out of his *WHAT IF?* scenario as the mysterious rider knocked his Light Cycle right into Beck's, trying to throw him off. Beck gripped the handlebars and held on tight as the rider leaned in for another jolt. Righting the wobble from each of the pursuer's knocks was making it increasingly hard to keep the cycle balanced on the unforgiving ice and its randomly integrated friction coefficient. In simpler terms, it was as slippery as anything, and the attacker's onslaught wasn't helping.

"You're still here?" Beck yelled over the howl of the wind. "Thought you gave up!"

The masked rider turned, his helmet shifting from opaque to transparent. Behind the now-clear visor, Tron looked stoically at Beck.

"You've got a lot to learn."

Beck scanned the field of ice and spied a fissure looming directly in his path. He smiled.

"Okay, old-timer. Teach me something."

Beck twisted the throttle full back and shot across the chasm. On the other side, he landed with relative ease, his rear wheel fishtailing only slightly on the ice. Somehow, the trailing light ribbon stabilized him on the treacherous terrain. Coherent light, indeed.

Beck smiled triumphantly, glancing back as Tron executed a flawless jump—minus any fishtailing. Ahead, another fissure broke the smooth continuity of the ice. Tron pulled alongside again.

"Stay focused, Beck," he shouted over the howling winds.

"*You* focus," replied Beck. "I got this."

This time, Beck and Tron jumped simultaneously, near mirror images of the other until the landing. Beck's rear wheel faltered again, the wobble more pronounced and harder to right this time. In the midst of regaining control, Beck was happy he landed at all, instead of wiping out.

Of course, Tron's landing was again error-free.

"Close call," said Tron.

Beck was about to offer a retort when he saw a canyon up ahead. The previous fissures were nothing compared to the seemingly bottomless pit yawning wide to swallow them up.

Despite his bravado, Beck hesitated.

Tron showed no such pause. He raced ahead, his Light Cycle kicking back tiny chips of ice, which frosted Beck's visor, briefly obscuring his vision. Beck wiped the visor and watched awestruck as Tron aimed straight for the canyon and soared across in a majestic arc, landing safely on the other side.

Beck steeled himself for his decision: If Tron could do it, so can I.

Beck hit the accelerator and shot forward, soaring across the abyss. But even as his rear wheel broke contact with the ice at the edge of the canyon, Beck knew that he wasn't going to make it. His Light Cycle started to fall. His hesitation had cost him too much forward momentum.

"Beck!" Tron yelled from the other side.

Beck had no time to respond. He let go of the Light Cycle and pushed himself away from it. In an instant, the plummeting Light Cycle deactivated, irregular planes collapsing upon themselves as the cycle folded back into a baton. His arms pinwheeling, Beck reached out, desperate to catch it, but his gloved fingertips just grazed the baton before it disappeared into the depths.

A few meters shy of the opposite side, Beck's momentum sent him crashing against the canyon wall, mostly craggy ice broken into fractals. Beck struggled to grab a narrow handhold, but the shard of ice crumbled. He slid further down the wall, gloved fingers digging in as he reached for *anything* to halt his descent into the abyss. He finally stopped by jamming a glove into a crack and balancing a boot precariously on an outcropping only slightly less fractious than the first. He couldn't stay there for long.

Beck nearly lost his tenuous grip, but just then a rope dropped beside him. He looked up. Tron had rappelled down into the canyon.

Beck reached out and made sure the line was taut, and then he began to climb up and out of the canyon with Tron's help.

"You know what you did wrong?" said Tron.

"Yeah, I followed you," Beck replied.

"You hesitated. I didn't," said Tron.

At the lip of the canyon, a ledge of ice jutted out precariously. Tron made his way up and over it, climbing without hesitation.

Beck had a harder time, attempting two approaches before finally making it over the ledge, which strained under his weight. Just as he cleared the obstacle and stood on firmer footing, the ledge crumbled into gemlike fractals that followed Beck's lost baton down into the abyss.

Tron removed his helmet and offered Beck a wan smile, but it was little consolation.

"How can I be 'the next Tron' if I can't even keep up with the *real* one?" said Beck as he removed his own helmet. Instantly he felt the raw chill from the relentless wind scouring the Outlands.

Beck kicked a loose chunk of ice and it went skittering off into the gloom.

"You need to have faith in yourself if you want to inspire hope in others," said Tron.

"Easy for you to say. You were programmed to protect the Grid. I was programmed to tune up engines. And it looks like I wasn't even very good at that."

Tron clapped Beck on the shoulder.

"You're *more* than just a mechanic, Beck. You surpassed your programming. You stood up for what you believed in, all on your own. The uprising needs a hero like you."

Beck looked around. He saw nothing but ice and digital desolation in every direction.

"What uprising? It's just you and me out here."

Tron took a deep breath. He knew Beck had potential, he just needed Beck to see it, too.

"Aren't *you* the one who said others will follow? That the revolution will spread if we ignite the spark?"

Beck just shook his head. "You're listening to me now? I almost plunged into the bottom of a canyon. You risked your own life to save me. I don't think I'm cut out to inspire anyone. Sorry."

Beck turned away from his mentor, despondent.

"Beck," said Tron.

Beck didn't answer.

"*Beck*."

"What?"

"Your baton?"

Beck turned and gazed down into the gaping abyss.

"You should probably get that," said Tron.

"But I'm going to be late for work!" said Beck, turning just in time to be hit in the face with a glowing coil of rope.

The rope slipped toward the edge of the canyon. Beck snatched it up before it disappeared. He sighed.

"Right."

CHAPTER 2

BECK DIDN'T HESITATE, but he rode his Light Cycle out of the Outlands with more caution than usual. Nearly getting derezzed was sobering enough. Having to rappel alone into an uncharted ice canyon to retrieve his baton frayed his nerves even more.

Tron cast a long shadow, but the Grid's legendary protector was long gone when Beck climbed back out of the hole he had effectively made for himself. Lucky for Beck, the canyon did, in fact, have a bottom. There, deep down in pitch-blackness, Beck retrieved the baton as a low growl echoed ominously through the crags. He thought it might just be the howling winds of the Outlands, not some rogue primordial program hiding down there in the darkness. Nevertheless, Beck got out of that hole as fast as he could climb.

Now, racing from desolation toward the shimmering lights of Argon City, Beck allowed himself to smile at the thought of home.

Near the city limits, Beck spotted a checkpoint. There were more and more these days. Moving in and out of Argon was becoming as dangerous as plowing across ice at full-throttle.

Beck deactivated his cycle and scanned for nearby cover, some boulder to crouch behind . . .

Beck stiffened as a spotlight beamed down on him. He looked up, pupils dilating in the glare. The light shone from a Recognizer hovering silently and stealthily at the edge of the city. *Busted*.

"HALT, PROGRAM! YOU ARE OUTSIDE THE AUTHORIZED ZONE!" Boomed a voice from above.

"Great. Now I'm *definitely* late for work. This just gets better and better." Beck sighed.

As the Recognizer landed, its ramp descending like the lapping tongue of a mechanical predator, Beck sprinted off. Armed Sentries spilled out of the Recognizer's ramp, running after him.

This wasn't the first time Beck had to elude the patrols. He doubled back and crisscrossed over his tracks to throw off the Sentries. They expected a linear path to pursue. Beck gave them anything but, at turns retreating toward the Outlands before aiming squarely back into the general direction of Argon City.

It wasn't long, though, before Beck was out of breath. He crept up to a newly erected structure and hid in the shadows as a small phalanx of Sentries raced past. Beck held his breath.

"I THINK HE WENT THAT WAY!"

Beck exhaled, quietly.

The Sentries disappeared into the darkness. Most of the Sentries . . .

Beck heard more voices approaching and looked around the structure, desperate to find a deeper corner. Instead he found a door. Beck slipped inside, pulling the heavy hatch closed behind him without making a sound.

Beck sighed, more audibly this time, and looked around.

What he saw froze him in his tracks.

Beck found himself in a chamber filled with programs

huddled together in the dark, all of them chained to one another. As the door closed, he realized the mistake he had made.

"Please tell me you're hiding, too."

Beck's words were punctuated by the start of a rumbling ignition. The entire chamber thrummed in time to the vibrating engine. *No, not a chamber . . .* Beck sighed. "We're trapped, aren't we?" he said.

None of the chained programs responded. Beck wasn't going to wait for confirmation. He tried the door. Locked. He banged his shoulder against it. The hatch didn't budge. They were sealed in tight. Beck rested his forehead against the source of his misery, presently impenetrable. Outside he could discern a buzzing speaker-box Sentry.

"PROCEED WITH TRANSPORT."

Beck turned and slid to the floor of the transport, sitting on his rump. He thumped the back of his head against the reinforced wall, thinking. "This can't be good," he said.

One of the captured programs stood up and stepped forward. He offered Beck one of his hands bound tightly by glowing manacles. The gesture was well-meaning, even though Beck could hear the sarcasm in his voice.

"Congratulations, Program. You just made yourself a prisoner."

Beck shook his hand anyway.

"And you are?" inquired Beck.

"Cutler. Consider me the last friend you'll ever make."

CHAPTER 3

BECK HAD WALKED right into the enemy's hands.

Tron would never have done that.

"The next Tron"? Not so much . . .

Beck had scurried right into the back of a prisoner transport truck, which had in turn rolled without hesitation into a Recognizer. Inside the Recognizer, the truck disgorged its contents before armed Sentries who threw every last program—Beck included—into immobilizing restraints. They were all ushered into a cargo pod, which was transparent on all sides. The Recognizer soared high above Argon City. There was nowhere to go but down.

Still . . .

"Okay, who's for getting out of here?" offered Beck.

None of the other programs responded.

"Don't all jump up at once."

One of the prisoners, a tense young program named Rilo, spoke up.

"You *can't* get out of here. And if you try, you'll only get us into more trouble," said Rilo.

Cutler advanced from the tangle of prisoners.

"Cool it, Rilo."

"*Cool it*? Have you forgotten where they're taking us? Each one of us is going to end up derezzed! Have you ever seen anyone get derezzed? It's not pretty!" As Rilo seethed, his words spawned a murmur of fear that passed along from prisoner to prisoner like a virus. Even Beck was unnerved, and he *had* seen someone derezzed before.

"What's he talking about? Where are we going?" said Beck.

Rilo's fear was infectious. He was, as they say, bugging out.

"Tell him, Cutler. Tell him where they're taking us!"

Cutler stared grimly out the window. Why say it? Everyone else knew. Everyone but Beck.

Beck pushed past Rilo and stared out the transparent hull of the Recognizer's cargo pod. Far off, a massive coliseum could be seen rising out of an artificial island nestled in the Sea of

Simulation. Though covered in scaffolding and only half constructed, the Coliseum was a sight to behold. From concept to completion, it was envisioned to be the grandest structure built in this part of the Grid, a solid and authoritative structure.

Beck's bravado drained as quickly from him as the color left his face.

"The Games."

Beck sat down. He pondered what Tron might do. *Tron would win.*

But he knew the harsh reality was that he *wasn't* Tron.

Whoever believed he was "the next Tron" might do well to keep looking, Beck thought.

CHAPTER 4

AS BECK FACED HIS WORST NIGHTMARE, his friends went on with their lives, blessedly unaware. Beck worked in a garage, but it wasn't just any old repair shop. Able's Garage was *the* place in Argon City for repairs and upgrades. The garage's small staff was made up of the best programs around. Maybe not the most disciplined . . . but the best. The main staff was made of Beck, and his friends Zed and Mara. Of the three, Beck was the most likely to get in over his head, which is why Mara was worried when he didn't show up for work. . . . Zed was less observant. He did his best work at night, undisturbed by random programs that used and abused their vehicles without any basic understanding of how they functioned. Zed worked at tuning up a Light Cycle. He knew nothing of Beck's plight, but he couldn't shake the feeling that something was not right.

Zed labored in the shadow of a Light Jet parked nearby. Mounted on the airship's cockpit was a monstrous gun turret. Zed focused on his work, oblivious to the turret pivoting to point directly at the back of his head. Just then, Mara popped out of the cockpit, wiping a few beads of sweat from her brow with the palm of her hand.

"Finally! It has taken me *forever* to get this thing working—"

Mara looked down and saw the turret poised to blast Zed into a fine, pixilated mist.

"Oh, whoops. Sorry, Zed."

"Sorry for what?" said Zed, not bothering to turn around.

Mara repositioned the turret, aiming it away from the back of Zed's head. Zed didn't look up. He was none the wiser. That was Zed. Very good at his job, but not the brightest light in the group.

As she made final adjustments to the turret, Able— the proprietor of Able's Garage—walked in. He looked irritated. Invariably, Able's irritation was directed squarely at Beck, or at the others in reference to Beck when Beck wasn't around, which these days was more often than not.

"Did Beck even bother coming in today?" growled Able.

Zed and Mara exchanged glances. They had, over time, developed an unspoken code in order to provide convenient if not watertight alibis for their friend. Sometimes they got their lines crossed.

"I'm sure he's just taking a break," said Zed.

"I thought I saw him working in the flight bay," said Mara at the same time.

Able snorted a little as he exhaled. It was his way of showing his employees—the ones keeping regular hours, that is—that he was *unconvinced*.

"Well, it's his loss. I was going to let him tune up one of my bikes. My *favorite* bike, actually."

Able held up a sleek baton and then tapped it against the heel of his boot with a flourish. A classic Light Cycle appeared from the baton. Sleek lines, but definitely retro. It was an older version than the compact, uniform models displayed in the workroom. Neither Zed nor Mara had ever seen anything like it.

"Whoa," whispered Zed, wide-eyed.

Mara was equally awestruck, but managed to breathe.

"They don't make bikes like that anymore. Where'd you get it?"

Able laid a hand to the side of mouth and leaned forward conspiratorially after quickly glancing around to see if anyone else was around. They were alone in the garage, machine-heads all. Able lowered his voice, but spoke casually, as if his matter-of-fact revelation was an everyday occurrence.

"From Flynn."

Zed and Mara nearly jumped back as if jolted. Mara first regained enough composure to speak.

"Flynn? KEVIN FLYNN?"

Zed ran his hand along the gentle slope of the Light Cycle's canopy. It was almost a caress. "The Creator? He gave you this bike?!"

Able stooped to fuss at a spot on the Light Cycle, a minor blemish that seemed to have trouble keeping rez and color to match the rest of the cycle's decor. The garage owner spat on his thumb and rubbed.

"He owed me a small favor. But that was a long time ago. Things were different," he said and deactivated the Light Cycle. They had heard this nostalgic tone in Able's voice before, but no one knew what to say.

Flynn's bike collapsed into its baton. Able gripped it tightly as he began walking away.

"Can you let Beck know it's in my office?" he said softly.

Zed and Mara each nodded.

"I hope he's not getting himself into any trouble," said Able as he rounded the corner and disappeared from view.

When Able was safely out of earshot, Mara whistled softly and climbed down from the Light Jet.

"Able *knew* Flynn, can you believe it?"

Despite her mechanic's gear and a smudge of dark digital lubricant across the bridge of her nose, there was no mistaking Mara's beauty. Zed stared at her. In mixed company, he was able to focus his feelings elsewhere. But here, alone and just the two of them, Zed had trouble hiding his crush on her.

"Zed?"

Mara snapped her fingers scant millimeters in front of Zed's nose. Zed blinked several times and came back to reality.

"What? Oh, sorry. I'm just . . ."

"Just what?" Mara asked.

"Just worried about Beck. That's all."

Mara touched Zed's arm. It was the best thing that happened to him all day.

"I'm sure he's fine," she said. "You, on the other hand, look like you could use a break."

"I do?"

"You've been working really hard. Don't think I haven't noticed."

"You have?"

Mara glanced at her reflection in the Light Cycle Zed was tuning up. She wiped away the smudge on her nose.

"Sure. I'm sure this cycle is at optimum performance now. You, however . . ."

Zed stared. Mara took him by the arm.

"Come on, it's nothing the club can't cure. What do you say? You and me—"

"You mean . . . just *us*?" said Zed.

"Don't look so nervous, Zed," she led him out of the garage.

Zed thought of all his imagined subroutines. In all the scenarios he played out, he had somehow omitted this one.

"Beck?" he said.

"I'm sure Beck can take care of himself."

CHAPTER 5

INSIDE THE COLISEUM, which somehow seemed larger within than without, Beck awaited his fate. While the structure's exterior was massive, and would be even *more* massive once completed, the interior space seemingly defied ordinary spatial rules. "How better to cram in spectators for this circus," he muttered.

The other prisoners gazed warily at Beck.

Their numbers had been culled down to a group of just several male programs—five total, Rilo and Cutler among them— each now bound by ankle restraints to a circular platform. Everything else beyond the platform's perimeter was blinding, intense light. Rilo spoke, his voice quavering as before, not a vocal glitch but his own palpable fear untethered.

"This is wrong. I shouldn't be here. I didn't do anything. It's all the renegade—"

The intense light suddenly waned, muting to a warmer and less threatening brightness befitting the quartet of Sirens that emerged.

The Sirens' primary, a statuesque beauty with hair shimmering like copper, touched Beck's chest. It felt electric. Instantly, his mechanic's uniform shifted, reforming into a neon blue battlesuit. She tapped Beck's shoulder with a well-manicured fingernail and the numeral **5** appeared on his shoulder in lighted relief. It glowed brightly.

"Rilo, I told you. It's not—" Cutler began, but Rilo cut him off.

"His fault?" Rilo hissed.

Cutler frowned. The Sirens paused, freezing in place and watching them curiously. Rilo continued, speaking to Cutler, but casting sidelong accusatory glances at Beck.

"The only reason we're here is because the renegade 'remodeled' Clu's statue. Next thing I know, they pick me up for breaking curfew. *Curfew.* I lost track of time. I shouldn't have to *die* for it."

Beck sighed with guilt. *He* was the renegade everyone was talking about. He had destroyed Clu's statue and eluded General Tesler's patrols. Tron had given him sanctuary in the Outlands, and it was there that Beck had begun training to be the next Tron. But Tron was the most hunted program on the Grid, and Beck knew that secret was more important than his own life—than *all* of their lives. He tried his best to comfort Rilo and appear calm, as Tron had earlier done for him.

"We'll survive this. You're not going to die," he said.

"You got that right," said Cutler. "I'll derez *ten* of them before they figure out who they're supposed to be fighting."

Rilo shook his head in despair. "There's *ten* of them?"

The Sirens returned to their work, touching each of the other prisoners, their clothing shifting into armored battlesuits. Cutler looked down at his number: **3**. Apparently, the Sirens worked in reverse order. *A countdown, but to what?*

"If I don't survive, that renegade is to blame. Make no mistake," said Rilo, glaring daggers at Beck.

One of the Sirens tapped Rilo on his shoulder and the numeral **1** glowed to life. He closed his eyes and lowered his head as if dejected.

"Processing complete. Proceeding to Games," said the primary Siren, stepping back, as did her sisters, retreating into the halo of light once more.

As quickly as the Sirens departed, the platform upon which Beck and the prisoners stood began to rise, ascending toward a ceiling that unfolded to reveal an iridescent elevator shaft. The elevator tube glowed to life as if to entreat them inside. Rilo shuddered. Cutler, however, seemed pumped up with anticipation.

"Well," he said, "here's our chance to fight back."

They stepped aboard. There was no turning back. The elevator rocketed up and Beck struggled against the momentary vertiginous feeling, weightless for just an instant. And then the gravity of the situation became all too clear.

Beck stared in awe. The sound of the crowd was deafening. They were arrayed at the center of the giant space within the tesseract that comprised the Coliseum's interior. The structure was bigger on the inside than the outside. The prisoners stood dead center on a floating platform orbited by thousands of cheering spectators in free-floating gyroscopic stands that followed the action wherever it led: up, down, or sideways, the playing field in three deadly dimensions. There was, in point of fact, no bad seats in the entire house. You paid to see a show, and that's what you got—gladiatorial combat, up close and personal. Winner leaves, loser gets derezzed. End of line.

Across the expanse, another platform floated into view. Upon it stood an equal number of gladiators, their battle-suits glowing orange. The gladiators were Tesler's hand-picked Black Guards, their skills honed in countless hours of practice and made more keen by a string of uninterrupted wins in the Coliseum. These were the best of the best.

One of the gladiators hurled his disc at the crowd. Beck and Cutler tracked the disc's trajectory as it careened off a gyroscopic stand and ricocheted to and fro against the interior sidewalls of the Coliseum. Rilo cowered as the disc zoomed past the prisoners' platform before cutting across the null space back toward its thrower. The Orange gladiator reached up and caught his disc without even looking. The crowed roared its approval well before the disc alighted upon his fingers and settled back into the Orange fighter's merciless grasp. The gladiators were battle-hardened heroes to the crowd, and they loved the attention and adulation.

Rilo shot Beck a frightened look and moved closer to another prisoner, putting distance between himself and Beck.

"So, still think we're going to survive?" he called.

Rilo's final word seemed to echo within the cavernous Coliseum as the crowd hushed in unison, as if the air were sucked out of the room. A much more elaborate stand floated down from its high perch. Beck looked up and saw General Tesler, the program he hated most on the Grid. Tesler was one of the inner cabal who served the whims of Clu. And Clu was the tyrant who ruled the Grid. Made by the Creator himself, Kevin Flynn, Clu's intent was to oversee the Grid as its primary administrator, aided and abetted by Tron. However, Flynn had—in his haste (and perhaps with a bit of hubris)—made Clu in his own image. Clu's function was to create the perfect system as deemed by Flynn. But Clu's zeal led to imposing order everywhere. And that meant controlling EVERYTHING. When Clu turned on his master, Flynn became a ghost in the machine, and the Grid devolved into a police state. Maintain Clu's idea of order and you were fine. But if you were a program with an independent thought? Well, start counting the cycles until you eventually got derezzed. . . .

Tron tried to do something about it, and Clu severely damaged the venerable program in return. So Tron set out to find "the next Tron," an able hero who just might have the spark to transcend his programming and do what others, including Tron, had failed to do: upend Clu and return the Grid to what it needed to be, a place of *peace*, where all were welcome.

Beck wondered what Tron would think of that future if he saw Beck now, right smack-dab in the lion's den.

Behind Tesler stood Paige and Pavel, Tesler's own loyal lieutenants. Paige had distinguished herself as a field commander and unparalled combatant. As for Pavel, Beck knew less about him. He was dangerous to *everyone*, Paige included. Pavel would do just about anything to rise to the rank of general himself, to sit at the right hand of Almighty Clu. Clu himself appeared as a glowing avatar behind the trio.

Beck watched as Tesler raised his hands dramatically. Clearly, the general was luxuriating in his audience, captive or not.

"In the name of our great leader, Clu . . . LET THE GAMES BEGIN!"

Beck braced for what would come next. Rilo moved behind

Cutler, choosing discretion over valor. All of them eyed the floating platform full of gladiators as it floated closer, their own platform edging forward to meet them.

As the gap between platforms diminished, one of the Orange gladiators raised his hand. The other gladiators watched him with anticipation. Beck singled him out as their leader—or perhaps the most eager to die.

"We're not going to last against the Black Guard," Rilo said.

At a remaining gap of just a few meters, the platforms ceased forward movement.

"Regiment! Position!" shouted the Orange leader.

The gladiators moved in unison, removing their discs from their backs and holding them perfectly poised as they took offensive stances.

"Those aren't prisoners . . ." began Cutler.

"We're not going to survive *two* rounds against those guys!" said Rilo.

Rilo clutched his disc in a shaky hand.

"Stick close to me, Rilo," said Beck. He knew that Rilo's angry attitude came from fear. Fear of losing, of being derezzed. Beck needed to keep Rilo *safe*. Maybe that's what being "the next Tron" did you to you—altruism trumped self-preservation. *Fight instead of flight.*

"ATTACK!" howled the Orange leader as he leaped toward the prisoners' platform, his regiment of gladiators following close behind.

Beck stole the quickest of glances skyward at General Tesler, but it was Paige who caught his attention.

What was that look in her eyes? Anticipation? *Or something else . . . ?*

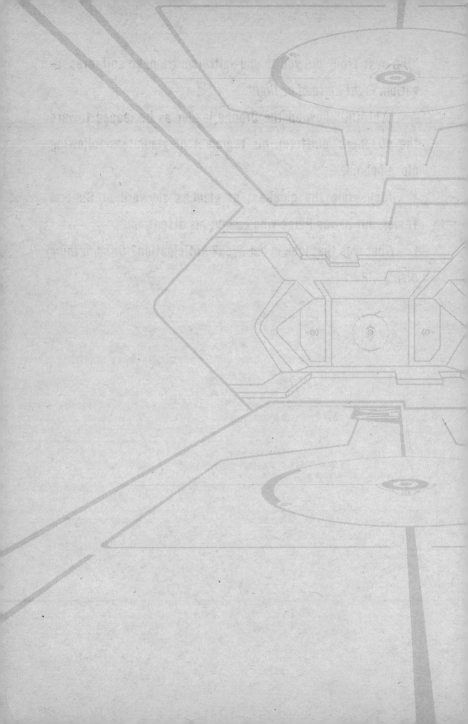

CHAPTER 6

ELSEWHERE, NEAR THE COMMERCE DISTRICT of Argon City, the 0001001 Club thrummed with thunderous dance beats.

Inside, Zed and Mara mingled among the other programs. A dance floor floated above the throng. Occasionally, Clu's Sentries would enter the club to spot-check for rogue programs. Then, the syncopated beats of whatever was playing were drowned out by the thudding boots of the Sentries.

"Oh, I *love* this song!" yelled Mara.

She took Zed's hand and dragged him up the free-floating steps that led to the dance floor.

"You know, I'm not really much of a dancer! Are you thirsty?" Zed called, hooking a thumb back to one of the drinks stations on the primary floor.

Mara ignored him and stepped onto the dance floor, joining the gyrations of the rest. Zed backed down the floating stairs, wishing that his dance moves matched his skills calibrating Light Cycles.

"A drink? Oh, yeah, sure." Mara shrugged and continued dancing.

Zed headed for the closest bar, one manned by a program known as Shaddix. Zed had struck up a passing friendship with Shaddix during all the times he had begged off dancing, preferring instead to prop up the bar rather than embarrass himself with his admittedly pitiful dance moves.

"Hey, Zed. The usual?" said Shaddix.

"Two, please," replied Zed.

Shaddix mixed liquids from two bottles into a pair of tumblers. The liquids, inert separately, mixed into an energized solution that glowed in the dim light of the club. Shaddix added sparkling polymer straws to each and handed the drinks to Zed. He took a sip of his own before turning to look for Mara.

"Great. Just great," he muttered aloud to himself.

Zed watched as Mara was surrounded by four handsome

young programs, none of them mechanics or denizens of any of the service castes. Each of them jockeyed for Mara's attention, and—by Zed's estimation—she was clearly *enjoying* their efforts.

Zed slumped back into a stool at Shaddix's station, crestfallen. He took another sip of his drink and set Mara's down on the bar.

"Is this for me?" purred a soft voice.

Zed looked up at an attractive female program standing beside him. In all his mooning over Mara, he didn't notice her approach. She took Mara's drink from the bar and sipped it. Zed stared.

"What? Oh . . . no," Zed stammered, shaking himself out of the fugue that now seemed to be induced not just by Mara, but *any* pretty program that sauntered his way.

Zed looked back at Mara. The entourage vying for her affection had grown from four to six young male programs dancing in a ring around her. So Zed turned to the program at his side. "Sure," he said, "it's all yours."

She stood, waiting for Zed to ask her to sit, but he missed every cue. Zed could diagnose a Light Cycle's maladies by each audible knock or ping, but understanding females was beyond his programming.

"Mind if I take a seat? I'm not much of a dancer." She nodded at the dance floor and the gaggle of programs.

Zed swallowed hard, tongue-tied. Young, pretty, *and* as averse to dancing as he was. If she started talking about Light Cycles, Zed was likely to faint dead away, system shutdown. Zed looked to Shaddix, *desperate*.

"It's all yours," said the bartender, as anxious to put Zed out of his misery as he was to be in as close proximity to the pretty program. Zed nodded quickly, mouthing 'thanks' to Shaddix as she sat down next to him, extending her hand.

"I'm Perl."

"This is Zed," said Shaddix.

Zed shot Shaddix an annoyed look.

"Thanks. I got it from here," he said, regaining his voice.

He shook Perl's hand, unaware that he was blushing brighter than the glow of the circuitry on his clothing.

On the dance floor, Mara stole another glance at Zed. She had been keeping track of him all night, even with the growing swarm of male programs dancing to get her attention. She could see that Zed and this pretty young program were hitting it off. Something more than jealousy made her concerned, but she couldn't quite put her finger on what. . . .

A short while and one private booth later, Zed's confidence had grown by leaps and bounds.

"So the third Siren says, 'I thought that disc looked familiar,'" said Zed as he finished one of the jokes in his small repertoire.

Perl cracked up at the punchline, laughing giddily.

"I love a program with a sense of humor," she said.

Zed responded by scanning the club for Mara, ultimately finding her at a bar surrounded by a group of male programs, likely the ones who won or placed in the dance-off for her attention. He gestured to her: *come over*. And then he trained his attentions fully upon Perl again. Mara sighed in frustration then pardoned herself from her admirers and walked over to the booth. She put a hard hand on Zed's shoulder. Though as small and lithe as Perl's, Mara's fingers were uncannily strong, as one would expect from a mechanic used to slinging spanners. She looked right at Perl.

"Mind if I borrow him?"

Perl smiled wanly and stared back at Mara.

"Just bring him back in one piece," said Perl.

Mara dragged Zed out of the booth, and when they were out of earshot—even without the aural overlay of driving beats—Zed leaned in close to speak. He was positively giddy—very *un*-Zed-like.

"Did you hear that? I don't even know what it means, but it sounds . . . *wild*."

"What are you doing? I thought we were hanging out?" said Mara over the cacophonous thump of another dance tune.

"We are," said Zed

"Zed, I haven't seen you all night. Except on the arm of that pretty young thing. What is she? An unemployed Siren? You left to get a drink and never came back."

Zed's giddiness soured to sarcasm. "You looked busy."

Mara recognized the shift in his mood.

"Well, I was killing time waiting for you. Come on, let's dance," she said.

"Dance? You and me?"

"Of course, Zed. You and me."

Zed's spirits soared and he all but forgot about Perl, who

watched the interchange with great interest from the booth. Maybe, Zed thought, just *maybe* Mara had feelings for him after all . . . and not for whatever handsome young program that danced across her path.

"Zed, c'mon, we're friends, aren't we?"

Zed's soaring spirits crashed into some invisible, impenetrable barrier and derezzed into tiny dying sparks.

"Right. Friends," said Zed.

He looked back at Perl, who winked mischievously. What Zed didn't realize was that Perl was winking to Mara: *I win.*

"You know what, Mara? I'm sort of busy. Sorry."

Zed brushed past Mara and returned to the booth.

"You want to get out of here?"

"*Absolutely*," said Perl.

They headed for the exit. Zed was thinking forward, not wanting to look back at Mara, who was more than a bit confused by the turn of events. Perl obliged, offering an innocent shrug and mouthing a remorseless 'sorry' to Mara as the door to the club slid shut behind them.

As a waiter program passed by, Mara snatched a drink

off his tray and downed the shimmering liquid in a single gulp. She deposited the empty at the bar and made her way back to the dance floor.

"Guess I'll see you later, Zed. . . ."

CHAPTER 7

A DIFFERENT KIND OF DANCE took place across town.

Inside the Coliseum, the Orange team was on the attack, hurling discs and charging at the Blue team of captured prisoners. The Blues were on the run. All except Beck, that is. Since the Orange platform had gravitated close to theirs, Beck knew that the only way to beat the opposing team of soldiers-turned-gladiators was to surprise them with a full-on assault. They expected all the Blues to turn tail and run. Not Beck. As a pair of Oranges closed in on Rilo, Beck dodged discs and parried blows with his opponents, surprising everyone with his speed and agility. When an Orange slashed out with his disc, Beck ducked low, sweeping the gladiator's legs with a swift kick that sent the enemy program tumbling right off the platform. The crowd was silent for a nanosecond, then roared its approval, applause reverberating throughout the Coliseum.

"Hey, that was *good*!" cheered Rilo, much surprised.

"We're gonna make it!" affirmed Beck, clapping Rilo on the back as they braced themselves for the next salvo from the Oranges.

Beck's bravery seemed to encourage Rilo. He stopped cowering, his spine stiffening. He even started fighting back. And that rallied Beck, too. An Orange gladiator came rushing at Beck, his disc swinging like a knife. Beck sidestepped a lethal slash and brought his own disc around in sweeping arc to score a deep cut in the Orange's forearm.

In the chaos, as Orange and Blue traded jousts between the two floating platforms, Beck got separated from Rilo. Hope for not just survival but victory itself seemed to enervate Rilo, who didn't see an Orange leaping behind him, disc punching out in a clenched fist.

"RILO!" Beck yelled.

But it was too late. Rilo didn't hear the warning over the din of the crowd, or the roaring, adrenalized pulses coursing through all the participants, Orange or Blue.

The Orange gladiator stabbed Rilo right in the back. The glow drained from Rilo and he shattered into a thousand digital cubes. Derezzed.

"NO!" Beck screamed, running to where Rilo had just stood. He slid through the cascade of cubes, which were themselves disintegrating into basic pixels, nothing but pinpoints of light.

Beck didn't see the Orange disc swinging toward his head.

"Get DOWN!" shouted Cutler, tackling Beck and sending both sprawling toward the edge of the platform, arms and legs akimbo.

Beck disentangled himself from Cutler and gave him a quick nod. *Thanks*.

Then he pushed himself to his feet, eyes welling with emotion. They're called *tears*, he thought. Pain. Sadness. Anger. *All of it*.

Beck lifted his disc and went charging for the Orange who had derezzed Rilo. Now all anyone in the Coliseum that night could hear was the cry of rage from a Blue whose name would fill the tesseract space to bursting and spill forth into Argon City and across the entirety of the Grid. . . .

The next Tron: *Beck*.

47

As Beck rushed toward Rilo's killer, a trio of Orange gladiators descended upon him from all sides, discs out and ready to derez. Beck slashed with his own disc, scattering the three dodging Oranges. He kicked the first one in the belly, sending him tumbling right off the platform. The second tried to slice Beck in half with an arcing sweep of his disc. Instead, Beck caught the Orange and spun him right around, the enemy's forward momentum sending him smashing disc-first into the third Orange. Derezzed. *Unfriendly fire . . .*

The Oranges were buzzing mad now and working to regroup as Cutler came rolling over to Beck's side.

"I couldn't save Rilo," said Beck. "He's gone."

Cutler punched Beck in the shoulder, snapping him out of his guilt. He pointed at the Orange platform, circling predatorily around the Blue team . . . or what remained of it.

"But we're not. And neither are *they*," Cutler said.

Beck watched as a hapless Blue tried to seek refuge on the Orange platform, leaping the gap and followed by two Orange gladiators working as a team, one cutting the Blue's path short, the other derezzing him.

Now it was just two Blues, Beck and Cutler.

"Let's level the playing field," said Beck.

The Orange platform floated around their field, turning on its own center of gravity, specifically from the weight generated by the two Oranges on its outer rim. As the platform moved vertical to Beck and Cutler's court, Beck took off running, leaping the boundless chasm. A hush fell over the audience. What was he doing?

Beck landed on the other side, taking the fight right to the Oranges. Offensive play by prisoners was almost unheard of in the Games. More often than not, the prisoner players just did their level best to avoid being derezzed. Not Beck, who was now at a right angle to game play. He ran up the center of the platform, allowing—momentarily, at least—a bird's-eye view of the Oranges below.

"Hello, down there!" Beck called from his high perch.

The Oranges looked up in time to see Beck's disc hurled down from above, grazing one of the gladiators' shoulders and banking over to clip a second Orange's wrist. So stunned were they by the sneak attack, the Orange gladiators dropped their discs.

That's when Cutler jumped into the fray.

Before the Orange with the shoulder wound could retrieve his disc, Cutler leaped the gap between platforms and derezzed him. Beck watched as Cutler kicked the Orange with the clipped wrist off the platform, which had begun its own erratic spin. The crowd went wild. Beck took off in the opposite direction, jumping the lip of the platform as it swung 'round. The second Orange was too busy trying to right himself on the topsy-turvy platform—just barely hanging on—to notice Beck now coming right for him as his platform completed its wobbly orbit.

"Where did you—?" stammered the Orange as Beck slid on his side, ducking and blocking a blow from the enemy gladiator. Beck jumped from the platform. The gladiator leaped after him, but he couldn't grab Beck's leg and fell toward the ground.

Above the action in the observation booth, General Tesler and his team watched grimly. Paige arched an eyebrow, intrigued by the turn of events. As the platforms collided with a jolt that reverberated throughout the null space, it was two-on-one now, the odds decidedly in Blue's favor as Beck and Cutler went after the remaining Orange. Minus his squad, his grace under fire had left him with all the suddenness of a system crash. More than anything, Paige appreciated a good challenge.

"They're good," said Paige.

"Too good," said Tesler.

The general turned to Pavel. "Sound the bell."

"But the round—" Pavel began to protest.

"Is over," said Tesler. "Do it."

Pavel acquiesced with a quick nod. To question the general's orders in the smallest way could mean demotion or derezzing, depending on Tesler's mood. And, apparently, the general's demeanor had turned as quickly as the tide of battle between the Oranges and these intriguing Blues.

"At once, sir," said Pavel, hitting an elaborate gong.

The Coliseum fell silent as intense vibrations swiftly echoed throughout the tesseract, then diminished as the null space absorbed the gong's resonating frequency.

"THIS ROUND OF THE GAMES WILL CONCLUDE *EARLY*," Pavel announced to the crowd.

The audience booed, first as a low murmur of disapproval, and then rising to a rumble of white noise that rivaled the gong ending play.

Tesler ignored the crowd's protestations, turning to exit the observation platform. Pavel waited a beat and then followed right on the heels of his master. Paige lingered just a bit, stealing a glance at Beck before departing also.

"What just happened?" said Cutler.

Beck and Cutler and a grateful Orange gladiator, last of his ranks, watched as Sentries appeared from all sides, weapons poised. The platforms were righting themselves, orbits decaying as the Sentries motioned for the Blues and Orange to follow.

"I'd say you two just got lucky," sneered the Orange, evidently emboldened now that the Games were called on account of . . . *what exactly?*

"Actually, I think *you're* the lucky one," said Beck, tapping the Orange on the nose with his disc.

The Sentries primed their weapons, training all guns on Beck.

"Somehow, I don't think you're going to use those," said Beck.

They followed the Sentries out of the arena. Cutler raised his fist to the audience before they exited and the crowd responded in kind.

CHAPTER 8

OUTSIDE THE CLUB, Zed was spiraling close to blowing it with Perl.

"So . . . do you want to take a walk?" he said.

Perl smiled. "We are walking."

Zed tried hard to remember a list of local activities he had scanned earlier—like he did every day—on the remote chance that he might find himself alone with Mara. Except that Mara was tripping the light fantastic back in the club with her adoring dance team. Zed, meanwhile, was here now . . . with the pretty program Perl.

"Right," said Zed.

He waited a beat.

"There's a cool light show at the park. . . ."

"Are you kidding me?" said Perl, bemused.

Zed scrolled through his mental list of *fun things to do with Mara*. . . .

"How about a bike ride on the Eastern Shore?"

Perl smiled wanly. Zed was losing her.

"My Light Cycle is acting up. Maybe another time," said Perl, stepping away.

"Wait—!"

Perl paused. In the dark of the night, Zed wasn't sure if what he saw—or *hoped* he saw—might actually be the smile that had made him momentarily forget about Mara back at the club.

"I can fix your bike," he said.

"You can?"

Zed's confidence was growing incrementally. After all, Perl wasn't walking away any more. In fact, she had sashayed *closer*.

"Sure. I work at Able's Garage. Only the best shop in Argon. We even do repairs for General Tesler. Military vehicles. Serious stuff."

Perl edged closer still, fingertips grazing Zed's forearm.

"Military tech, huh? Any weaponry?" she purred.

"Yes! Lots of big guns!" Zed fairly shouted.

Programs queued outside in the mist waiting to go into the club looked up at Zed's outburst. Perl led him away, out of the range of any curious ears.

"But it's late," she said. "The garage is probably closed."

"Probably." Zed smiled broadly. "So are you coming or not?"

The holding cells at the Coliseum were featureless trapezoids, crystal matrices grown large enough to hold a small group of prisoners until their eventual fate in the gladiatorial arena. Whatever elation had buoyed Beck's spirits on the gaming platform had evaporated. He sat alone with Cutler until the Sentries returned with a new group of prisoners clad in the same Blue battlesuits that they wore. Except Beck's and Cutler's still bore the slices and dices of the recent Games, called early on account of . . . What exactly? *Because we were WINNING . . .*

The new prisoners regarded Beck and Cutler warily. They had not yet heard the results of the night's Games. Legends, even in the Grid, were slow to build.

"We have new teammates to break in," said Cutler.

"You mean more programs to get derezzed in the next round," Beck replied. He got up and moved away from Cutler and the new prisoners. Cutler followed, not bothering to lower his voice. He had no secrets. Not from *any* program.

"Don't tell me you're giving up. We could use you out there. You're not a bad fighter. I mean, that maneuver on the rotating platform . . ."

"It was nothing. Just a fluke," said Beck.

"So it's like that, huh? No hope? I felt that way once. Just after we lost the ISO War."

"*You* fought in the ISO War?"

Cutler didn't answer. Beck watched as he traced a finger around a circular device, no larger than a watch face, banded upon Cutler's arm. The device suddenly illuminated, revealing the unmistakable symbol at its center: *the ISO sigil.*

Cutler was an ISO.

"You . . ." said Beck.

"I was just a foot soldier, nobody special. Most of my friends fell fighting Clu and his forces. To stay alive, I had to run away. Go underground. Pretend I was something I wasn't. Something

I was never meant to be. In all that, I almost lost myself in despair. . . ."

Beck waited. Cutler's admission had drawn the interest of the new prisoners.

"Until the *renegade* showed up," said Zed.

Beck felt his heart thunder inside his chest.

"The renegade. You heard Rilo. Isn't this all *his* fault?" said Beck.

Cutler traced the ISO sigil again with his fingertip and it disappeared. But they had all seen it. For Beck, it was stitched into the tapestry of his memory. Cutler met Beck's gaze.

"I don't think so. I think the renegade is doing good. When he blew up Clu's statue, I thought it was just a prank. But then I heard how he saved all those programs from the Games."

Beck tried to look away, but Cutler moved in front of him.

"If he's willing to risk his life to fight back," said Cutler, "then I want to be fighting right beside him. That's why I came to Argon. To join him."

Beck looked around the cell. He could think of nothing to express except to gesture at the irony of it. *WHERE they were.*

The invariability of luck that eventually runs out. Cutler continued his pep talk.

"But there's more. There's a reason I know it's all worth the risk," he said leaning close to Beck.

"I know who the renegade *really* is."

"Who?" muttered Beck. Had he been unmasked? Surely the Games were too chaotic for everyone to make such a leap in logic. . . .

"We both know. He's the one program who can save us all. Whose name alone inspires *hope*," said Cutler.

Beck swallowed hard. He had difficulty speaking above a croak.

"Who is he?" Beck said again.

Cutler grinned conspiratorially.

"He's *Tron*."

Beck races though the icy Outlands.

Beck and Tron talk strategy in the Outlands.

Forced to fight on the Grid, Beck battles against the forces of General Tesler.

General Tesler watches the fight in the Coliseum with great interest.

Cutler takes on the Grid's dangerous gladiators.

Beck's friend Mara is an expert mechanic.

Tron rides a Light Cycle designed to handle icy terrain.

Beck and his team prepare to fight for their lives in the Coliseum.

Paige leads two of the Black Guard in an attack.

An attack helicopter hunts for Beck on the streets of Argon City.

Paige leads General Tesler's forces, including hulking Sentries and giant floating Recognizers.

The original Tron begins to train Beck to free Argon City.

Beck is a fierce fighter with a disc, ready to take on the world!

The future of Argon City will be determined by the bravery of a few programs—especially Beck, the "new Tron"!

Beck, in his disguise as the new Tron, prepares to take on General Tesler's forces!

CHAPTER 9

WHEN ZED USED HIS PASSCODE to enter Able's Garage, all the interior lights were dimmed to energy-conservation mode. Able had gone upstairs for the night—and Zed thanked the Creator for that. Able may have been flexible in many ways, especially regarding Beck's mercurial notions of regular work hours, but he had one immutable rule: *no unauthorized programs around the vehicles.* Able ran a tight garage. His fixes were fast and done right the *first* time. And he could be discreet, which made his work sought after by both private citizens (if there was anything resembling privacy anymore), as well as Clu's security and military divisions. Unfortunately, it was harder and harder to distinguish between the two.

Inside the garage, as motion-activated lights came on with

each step, Perl looked around the collection of vehicles: Light Cycles in every design, Light Jets, Light Tanks, and various sundry military craft, most armed to the teeth with gun turrets or EM pulsers. Her wide, attractive eyes widened even further at the site of all that tech under one roof.

"I have to say . . ." she said, "this is kind of *cool*."

Zed watched her saunter between the tables of tools, fingers daintily feeling the various repair mechanisms. She inadvertently activated a light saw, which powered up with an energized hum that cut through the relative silence like its namesake. Zed hurriedly shut the saw back down, a single finger to his lips: *shhh . . .*

Zed pointed to a neon sign holographed to the wall adjacent to stairs ascending to the upper levels of Able's Garage: LIVING QUARTERS.

"There are programs upstairs," whispered Zed.

Perl shrugged. There was a mischievous glint in her eyes. Perl glanced at Able's office, its holographic warning stating simply (but *emphatically*, Zed knew): AUTHORIZED ENTRY ONLY.

"You're authorized, right? So it's okay to go in?" said Perl.

Zed's heart thundered. He was about to cross the Rubicon.

"I don't think that's such a great idea—"

Perl took Zed's hand in hers. Her touch was electric, seductive. She placed Zed's palm upon the ID lock, her smaller hand upon his. He wasn't sure if the tingling he felt, like static fuzz upon a monitor screen, was Perl's graceful touch or the vibrations of the scrolling scan mech as it verified the fractal whorls and lines of his palm and fingerprints.

"It'll be *our* secret," said Perl.

The door to Able's office slid sibilantly open. Perl laced her fingers around Zed's and entered, pulling Zed behind her.

Elsewhere, Beck and the other prisoners found themselves marched out of the Coliseum by a phalanx of Sentries. Their exit lacked the fanfare of the earlier elevator entry into the seemingly endless null space of the gladiatorial arena. Under cover of night, they were shunted out of the Coliseum and past the construction zone where the unfinished portions of the arena's exterior were still being built by mostly automated mechs. These were presently resting, dormant between shifts.

As a Light Truck passed, the Sentries didn't bother to halt

the procession, but merely girded the prisoners with raised weapons and the unspoken threat of violence if any attempted to escape. The truck hit a bump, some invisible flaw in the thorough-fare construct, and no one noticed a small metallic ring bounce out of the back of the vehicle. Nobody except Beck.

He feigned stumbling, surreptitiously palming and retrieving the ring as he caught his fall on the ground with a splayed hand.

"You okay?" Cutler turned back to look at Beck.

"I'm working on it," replied Beck.

He looked up at the scaffolding surrounding the exterior curve of the Coliseum, mostly a skeletal hull surrounded by powered-down cranes and construction machinery. Through the gaps in the ribbing of the Coliseum, he could just glimpse the Sea of Simulation in the distance. It was the only sign of any exterior feature—anything of the larger Grid world—beyond the towering walls. Beck paused just a bit, until a Sentry nudged him along with the end of his energy staff.

Beck leaned closer to Cutler as the chain of prisoners continued on.

"Tell the program in front of you . . ." said Beck, "TRON LIVES."

"What?"

"Just do it."

Cutler cast Beck a lingering look and then nodded. He turned to whisper to the prisoner in front of him. And that prisoner sent the message along, one to the next in a daisy chain relayed all the way to the front of the line.

"Tron lives? Who told you that?" said the leading prisoner, beginning of the line and corresponding end of the chain.

The Sentry at point turned to the leading prisoner.

"What was that?" growled the Sentry.

The prisoner stammered, "I . . . I . . ."

The Sentry raised his weapon. "Did you just say 'Tron lives'?"

All the prisoners clammed up. The Sentry halted the line abruptly. Like dominos, those further back—including Beck and Cutler—stopped short and jammed up against one another.

"I know what I heard," announced the Sentry for all to hear.

The Sentry began inspecting the ranks of prisoners, prodding each with his energy staff as if to elicit a confession.

"Talk like that is *sedition*. Who said it?"

The other Sentries watched the lead guard, perhaps waiting for one of the prisoners to step out of ranks and fall to his knees, begging for his life. With the Sentries' eyes everywhere but on him, Beck stepped back and flung the metallic ring he had retrieved at a nearby forklift. His aim was true. The ring struck the forklift's hand brake, and the forklift sprang to life. But even if someone were foolhardy enough to try to jump aboard, the fouled gears would prevent stopping what came next.

"Let's go," whispered Beck to Cutler.

The Sentries scrambled in confusion as the runaway forklift sent a heavy beam crashing down into their midst. Programs scattered. Motes of digital dust kicked up by the impact obscured what was swiftly turning into chaos. A pair of Sentries were knocked into the line of prisoners, a broken queue now, especially since Beck and Cutler had used the confusion to slip unnoticed into the skeletal scaffolding of the Coliseum. They were gone before the Sentries could manage a head count. With the forklift swinging to and fro, its hydraulic tines stabbing like the tusks of a mad beast, the Sentries had no choice but to put the thing down with a volley of coruscating bolts fired from their weapons.

By the time anyone realized that Beck and Cutler had escaped, they were long gone.

CHAPTER 10

IN A TRAINING SUITE IN MIDTOWN ARGON CITY, a masked warrior faced off against a horde of soldiers. The warrior was *surrounded*, and the combat—albeit on a smaller scale than in the Coliseum Games—would have been every bit as exciting if the participants used identity discs instead of simple nonlethal battle staffs and their own considerable martial-arts moves. These were General Tesler's elite.

The warrior launched a spin-kick into the closest soldier, boot colliding with his jaw and bowling him into two others. Three down, but only momentarily. As two more soldiers came rushing, the warrior met them with a cartwheeling kick to the first's midsection, a paralyzing blow to the solar plexus that crumbled the soldier into a gasping heap. The second was staggered by a simple but effective uppercut that broke his nose. The remaining soldiers closed in, leaving no escape for the masked warrior. . . .

Just then, a Sentry stepped inside and the soldiers stood down; those that had been knocked down picked themselves up and stood at attention with the rest. The masked warrior tapped the side of her helmet and the opaque canopy retracted, revealing General Tesler's aide-de-camp, Paige. She breathed deeply, not from exertion defeating soldiers much larger than herself, but from *annoyance*.

"This better be good," said Paige, meeting the Sentry.

The Sentry read a report scrolling upon the holographic array of his forearm comm.

"At first we thought it was a forklift accident. But then we did a head count. Two prisoners—"

Paige was headed for the door before he could finish.

"Ma'am . . ." began one of the soldiers.

Furious, but betraying no outward emotion, Paige snap-kicked him for good measure as she exited.

She was fairly certain without reading the prisoner manifest just which two prisoners had lighted out. And Paige knew beyond any shadow of doubt that General Tesler would have someone derezzed over the prisoner escape. She was going to make absolutely certain it wasn't *her*.

The construction zone at the Coliseum was a veritable labyrinth. After negotiating the complex web of scaffolding, Beck and Cutler had to surmount building materials piled into small and hazardous hills, minus hand- or footholds and threatening to collapse beneath them at any moment. The farside, beyond all the obstacles, left them momentarily crestfallen. It was a wall that looked insurmountable for two fleeing prisoners without any rope or climbing gear. One small grace was that the interior void of this wing had not yet been opened up into tesseract space. Then they might have been hiking for endless miles.

"End of the line," Cutler muttered, deflated.

"Not just yet," said Beck.

He scanned the interior gloom. There, just on the edge of visibility was a pipe conduit emerging from the wall. It was just big enough for each of them to crawl through, if not on elbows and knees then by inching along wormlike to the other side.

They squeezed through, just barely, Beck leading and Cutler craning his neck to steal glances back through the pipe's cramped pathway. He thought he heard the Sentries behind somewhere, overturning building materials in their haste to find the escapees. *Everyone*, not just the Sentries, knew the penalty for such transgressions. General Tesler was unforgiving. And Clu? Clu was utterly without mercy.

At the opposite end of the pipe, Beck breathed a sigh of relief. He gazed gratefully at the Sea of Simulation just a short distance away.

As Beck lowered himself to the ground, Cutler emerged from the tunnel.

"Look," said Cutler. "The bridge."

The Coliseum was settled on a small island connected to the mainland of Argon City by a glowing bridge that could accommodate a sizeable amount of both foot traffic and any make of vehicle conveying programs (or prisoners) to the Coliseum. With the games called short this night, the bridge was empty. No one and nothing coming or going. Beck smiled, then sprinted for the bridge. Cutler was grinning also, right on Beck's heels as they raced toward the foot of the bridge. Home free, Beck thought.

That was just before he saw figures emerging from the shadows of the bridge's enormous support struts.

Paige—back in uniform—blocked Beck and Cutler's path, a full platoon of Sentries flanking her. She held a length of light chain in one hand, the dragging links tinkling neon sparks upon the bridge's paving as she advanced toward the escaped prisoners.

"Why am I not surprised?" said Paige. She flexed her wrist, tightening her grip on the chain.

"You want to be a team? Then *be* a team," she said. She was determined to find out just how good these programs were.

Paige swung the chain overhead and hurled it outward like a bullwhip.

No, a lasso . . .

Beck realized his fate too late as the chain looped around his and Cutler's wrists, binding them together. Before the pair could struggle free, the Sentries were upon them, dragging them away.

The trip back to the Coliseum was far less dramatic than their flight. Shoved into—and not long after hauled out of—a transport, Beck and Cutler were summarily dumped onto the

Coliseum floor, well below the arena space occupied by the floating platforms they had earlier prevailed upon.

Cutler was the first to speak. "I suppose it could be worse," he said.

They were still bound at the wrists. Beck listened. The Sentries had gone. He could no longer hear their marching foot-falls. Instead, Beck registered a sound he knew as certain as his own breathing. Approaching motors revved, throttling up for maximum speed. A line of Light Cycles sped onto the Coliseum floor from a side ramp at the opposite side. Each bike made a hard-angle turn and raced toward Beck and Cutler, none slowing down.

"Oh, it's *worse*."

CHAPTER 11

THE INTERIOR LIGHTS OF THE COLISEUM flared to life as the Light Cycles came barreling toward Beck and Cutler, whose wrists were still shackled together.

"I guess the show wasn't over after all," Beck offered.

The line of Light Cycles was three riders deep and coming fast. Meanwhile, Beck and Cutler were on a steep learning curve figuring out how to move in tandem. They were no longer two separate programs but a unified being who stumbled over itself at every turn.

"Three of them, two of us. Those odds aren't so bad," said Beck. Cutler looked at him like Beck was a madman.

"But they've got bikes," replied Cutler.

Beck smiled. He had an idea.

"And we've got discs."

Cutler looked into Beck's eyes.

"Tron lives," said Beck.

"Tron lives," echoed Cutler.

The pair of reluctant compatriots nodded and grabbed their discs with their free hands. The Light Cycles were mere moments away.

"Now!" said Beck as they brought their discs down simultaneously on the chain binding them.

Nothing. No cut. No gouge. And no derezzing.

"Huh," chortled Beck. "I really thought that would—"

A cycle blew by and Beck leaped aside, but not fast or far enough to avoid the rider's outstretched fist. Beck's head spun around and he went down hard, dragging Cutler with him. The second rider bore down on Cutler, who tried to jump out of the way but was yanked backward by Beck, who was trying to flee in the opposite direction. Cutler hit the ground face-first.

"Move with me!" Beck shouted.

A second volley of riders entered the arena and rocketed toward them. Beck and Cutler dropped and rolled to avoid being rolled over themselves. But the chain tying their wrists only allowed so much movement. They ended up butting heads, stunning each other momentarily.

"Who needs them? We're killing each other!" growled Cutler as he nursed a twice-mashed nose.

The riders came around again, their engines droning out the cheers of the crowd as they got closer. Bruised and exhausted, Beck and Cutler watched as two of the riders disappeared down a ramp leading to a lower level of the Light-Cycle track. The floor, previously featureless and opaque, phased to transparency for the benefit of the audience. Not that it didn't help the hapless Beck and Cutler, too. They spied the riders crossing beneath them on the lower tier. The riders could be headed for any one of the transit tubes that would bring them zooming back onto the main combat floor and on a collision course with the prisoners. However, a more looming threat was the third rider, who executed a 180-degree burnout before cutting a swath toward Beck and Cutler.

"Do you trust me?" said Beck.

Cutler looked at him, concerned. They were swiftly running out of options, and they had already worn themselves out just trying to move in tandem without tripping each other up.

"Do I have a choice?" Cutler shot back.

The rider was almost on top of them, gunning his engine to create a burst of speed that shot his cycle forward. There would be no dodging him this time. Beck tightened his grip on the light chain around his wrist, taking it in both hands.

"When I give the word, pull as hard as you can," said Beck through gritted teeth.

Cutler looked down and understood. He did the same, grasping the chain with both hands as the rider revved.

"Keep still . . ." said Beck.

The rider wondered why these witless prisoners didn't get out of the way. Were they committing suicide? No matter, he thought. At the speed he was traveling, both would derez on impact and he would sail on through whatever tiny, disintegrating cubes remained in his wake. He gunned the cycle as fast as it would go.

"NOW!" yelled Beck.

Beck and Cutler dove in opposite directions, the light chain stretching taut between them and catching the rider at his midsection. His cycle kept going, but the rider was clotheslined, tumbling right off his vehicle.

The rider's bike skidded across the arena. The rider landed hard, his helmet slamming into the floor, rendering him unconscious. Within the arena, the silence was momentary, and then the crowd exploded with cheers.

"Tron lives." Cutler grinned.

"Come on," said Beck.

Below the transparent arena floor, Beck spotted another rider aiming for a spiral tube that would corkscrew the rider back to the central floor and right into the fray. Beck and Cutler ran full-tilt toward the corkscrew's terminal nexus.

"Now, DOWN!" yelled Beck.

Beck slid, dragging Cutler with him. The pair coasted in their battered battle suits toward the mouth of the ramp as the cycle surfaced, angling up and out of the corkscrew, catching air. It was all Beck and Cutler needed.

The pair slid directly beneath the airborne cycle, their chain outstretched as the cycle's ribbon of light came down synchronous to the cycle's descent. When the cycle's ribbon hit the chain, it severed in a sparking, shattering of illuminated links. They were free. And the crowd went wild.

As the third rider popped out of a nearby ramp, Beck and

Cutler separated. Cutler went off after the third, while Beck focused on the rider whose aerial maneuver had given the pair a new lease on life.

Cutler waited for the third rider to pass before hurling his identity disc. Unfortunately, the disc deflected off the Light Cycle's canopy. The rider braked hard, spinning his rear tires and kicking up a cloud of smoke as he caught traction and plowed forward again, headed back at Cutler.

Cutler spied his disc on the ground. It was too far away to retrieve in time. And then he looked down at the severed chain. The rider was approaching fast as Cutler took up the chain in both hands, swinging over his head like a lasso. The third rider, unsure what Cutler was attempting, leaned to the right and shot past as Cutler flung the chain with all his might.

Beck watched from some small distance away as Cutler's chain caught the rider by the throat, winding around his neck. But instead of pulling the rider off the bike, it yanked Cutler up and onto the speeding Light Cycle. Beck jumped back as the erratic cycle careened toward him, Cutler and its rider trading punches as Cutler held on for dear life.

Beck turned his attention back to the second rider, who

was veering toward him, his trajectory perpendicular to Cutler's runaway cycle. Beck held his disc in one hand and the remaining chain in the other. Neither were effective weapons. What he really needed to level the playing field was—

"A bike," said Beck. When the first of Tesler's riders fell, the Light Cycle changed back to its inert form, a small baton.

Beck raced for the baton, activating the Light Cycle as the second rider looped around. Beck fired up the engine, and his stolen cycle zoomed straight for the second rider.

"Now this is more like it!" Beck yelled into the wind.

He smiled as the second rider broke left and aimed for another corkscrew, spiraling down to the lower level. Beck followed, hot on his tail.

When the second rider popped out of the ramp on the lower tier, Beck had closed the gap between them. The second rider looked back, eyes wide. The rider broke into a zigzag motion, trailing a jagged light ribbon behind him. Beck leaned to the side, easily maneuvering around the hastily created obstacle course, past the ribbon of light. Beck sped forward until he was alongside his opponent.

"Bet you didn't know I'm a mechanic," he called out to the rider.

The rider responded by slamming his bike into Beck's, the impact from the caroming vehicles creating some breathing room. But Beck revved his engine in quick bursts, righting the wobble of his bike almost effortlessly and gliding back to the enemy rider, who was getting unnerved at Beck's cycle prowess.

"I'm a pretty good mechanic, too," Beck called out. Beck pulled out a mechanic's tool he and his friends used at Abel's Garage. By pressing the device against his foe's Light Cycle, he gained access to the bike's power supply. With a flick of the wrist, he cut power to the Light Cycle.

"Bye, now," said Beck, holding on to his cycle's handlebars with one hand and waving with the other, his severed light chain whipping in the wind.

The second rider's engine sputtered and then stalled, much to the terrified rider's chagrin. He went spinning out of control, tumbling tire-over-tire toward an embankment on the far wall. The rider bailed out just before his bike hit the wall, the vehicle derezzing on impact. Beck smiled, satisfied.

Cutler, meanwhile, had flipped around to the hood of his opponent's bike during their melee. They exchanged blows, fists, discs—even an errant kick or two—all at full-throttle as the rider tried to shake off Cutler. But it was a knock-down, drag-out battle for survival. And after surviving first the Games and then an escape attempt gone awry, Cutler wasn't about to give up now.

"Tron lives," Cutler spat through clenched teeth at the rider, who was glancing over Cutler's shoulder to the fast-approaching outer wall of the arena. The rider grinned evilly as he revved up. Cutler glanced over his shoulder and knew just where the rider was headed: *he was going to ram Cutler into the wall.*

Cutler tried to bail out, but his severed chain was still wrapped around the rider's throat, and the rider reached up to hold the chain tight. Cutler wasn't going anywhere.

He tried to punch his way loose, pummeling the rider with several hard blows and staggering him. Cutler stood up on the hood and ran up and over the rider, traversing the length of the bike in several desperate strides before leaping off the rear just as the bike hit the wall, this time shattering both the cycle and its rider into a million tiny cubes. Cutler's chain seemed to levitate in the air for a picosecond as the rider derezzed, and then its luminous links summarily clattered to the floor of the arena.

Cutler's momentum sent him sliding into the wall, too, but at much lower speed. No broken code, but it hurt. He turned from the wall to face an approaching cycle, willing—though not necessarily *ready*—to go another round. Thankfully, Beck was the rider. He screeched to a halt just scant millimeters from Cutler's twice-mashed nose. Beck extended a hand that Cutler gratefully accepted, climbing slowly to his feet. The two prisoners were startled by the thunderous applause from the spectators.

"Tron lives," said Beck.

"I'd say," said Cutler.

The energy in the arena surged even higher as Beck and Cutler raised their arms in victory.

Overhead, however, a storm surged.

Inside his private observation booth, the general stomped to the balcony and stared daggers at the crowd of energized programs. He was livid. And for General Tesler, such apoplectic displeasure usually meant someone got derezzed. In public, in private—it didn't matter as long as someone . . . anyone . . . *suffered*.

"Listen to them," growled Tesler.

Pavel and Paige stood a few feet behind the general. They eyed each other pensively.

"Cheering the actions of two conspirators," the general ranted. "This insolence will spread like a plague if we don't end it *now*."

He turned to face Pavel and Paige.

"So *end* it," said the general.

Paige did her best to mask her disappointment, but mostly she bowed her head and looked at her boots in humiliation. She had screwed up. *Big-time*. Bringing the conspirators—if they were, in fact, *truly* insurrectionists—back to the Coliseum could have gone any way. Martyrdom seemed least likely. But she didn't expect either of them to live, let alone become folk heroes.

"I take full—" she began, but Pavel cut her off.

"In all fairness to Paige, her plan *almost* worked."

Now it was Paige's turn to stare daggers, as Pavel worked hard to undermine her with the general and advance himself.

"May I suggest an *alternative*, general?" he said.

To Paige's great dismay, the general was all ears, waiting attentively as Pavel smiled his fatheaded leer and explained his idea in exacting detail. The general nodded with each point of the plot, and Paige began to realize that the winds of favor had shifted.

CHAPTER 12

INSIDE ABLE'S GARAGE, INSIDE *Able's office*, Perl picked up an object resting unobtrusively on Able's desk. Zed was getting more nervous with everything she touched—himself included. The object was a polyhedron that pulsed from a variably multi-sided shape to a simple square each time it responded to a closed question: **YES/NO**. Its name was Bit, and it predated Able himself. In fact, Bit was one of the first denizens of the Grid, older than Clu, programmed by the Creator himself. It was Flynn's widget, a piece of history. Zed knew that. But Perl didn't. And he wasn't volunteering any more information to Perl, who was very likely going to get him fired, tortured, or derezzed, not necessarily in that order.

"Careful. Some of this equipment is valuable."

"**YES**," stated Bit in a monotone corresponding to its monochromatic pixilation, polyhedron to cube and then back again.

"Looks like *junk* to me," said Perl.

"**YES**," affirmed Bit.

Perl smiled and tossed Bit aside as she wandered the confines of Able's office. It was a collection of parts and manifests piled high, resembling a junk shop more than a highly respected business.

"Well, it's getting kinda late. . . ." Perl shrugged, her curiosity dissolving to boredom.

Zed sensed that he was blowing his big opportunity. He was too inexperienced with girls to do more than stammer. Instead, he felt the need to impress Perl with what he knew—Light Cycles.

"Wait!" Zed rushed over to Able's desk and snatched up Flynn's baton. "Do you know what this is?" he said, showing it to Perl.

"A baton?"

"No. Well, *yes*. But do you know *who* it belonged to?"

Perl sighed and her wide eyes narrowed. Even Zed could see that she didn't expect to have to guess.

"This is Kevin Flynn's."

Perl's interest ignited again.

"Well, it was Flynn's, before he gave it to Able. Watch this—"

Zed activated the baton, and Flynn's sleek vintage Light Cycle emerged, seemingly out of thin air, filling the meager space left in Able's confined office. Perl had to edge close to Zed to make room for the classic bike. But her wide eyes lighted up, *sparkling*, which was exactly the reaction Zed had hoped for. She examined the bike closely, clearly impressed. And then she handed Zed her own baton while keeping one hand firmly on Flynn's.

"Think you can fix my bike like you promised?"

Zed took her baton and grinned eagerly.

"I'll have it singing in no time," he said, leaving Perl alone in Able's office.

With Flynn's Light Cycle.

Deep in the bowels of the Coliseum, Beck and Cutler sat at opposite ends—if you could call it that—of a cramped cell. The bravado they had displayed back in the arena had waned precipitously. Beck was beginning to think that being a prisoner was his new lot, an occupation certainly more exciting than being a mechanic, but with a much shorter life expectancy.

Cutler was the first to break the silence. "You put on quite a show out there. I'm impressed. You would have been a real asset during the war."

Beck snorted. If only Cutler knew the irony in his words . . .

"I doubt my involvement would've made any difference."

Cutler merely shrugged. "Anyone can make a difference as long as they keep fighting."

"You really believe that?"

"Don't you?"

Beck pondered that. He wondered if Cutler and Tron were conspiring to undermine his lack of confidence. Buoy his spirits. Raise him up.

Certainly, Cutler had more in common with the venerable hero than a mechanic with questionable judgment and a predilection to hesitate at the wrong moment did. Beck's head was swimming. Too many near-death jolts of adrenalized action and too little downtime to make sense of it all. He looked up as the cell door slid open to reveal a pair of Sentries. The Sentries stood at attention, then stepped aside—left and right—

to reveal a new addition to their captors: *Pavel*. Beck knew him by reputation only—a toady of General Tesler, ambitious to a fault. Pavel looked at Beck and Cutler with a mixture of contempt and indifference.

"Numbers three and five, follow me."

Beck and Cutler shared a glance: here we go again . . .

Elsewhere, Zed knelt beside Perl's bike, rearranging code and improving speed and performance capabilities with a surgeon's precision. Surely, his prowess in this regard would dazzle pretty, wide-eyed Perl. Mara at least appreciated Zed's way with vehicles despite his lack of social skills.

"You know, your bike's in decent shape. Like new. I actually can't find *anything* wrong with it."

Perl didn't respond.

"Perl?"

Zed tapped a switch and Perl's bike folded back into sheer planes of light and disappeared into her baton.

Zed looked around the dimmed garage. Even with the lights on conservational mode, he could see that he was alone.

"Perl, where'd you—?"

Just then a blue glow materialized out of the darkness. Zed turned in time to see Perl astride Flynn's vintage Light Cycle.

"Wait! Don't—"

He caught her smile and mischievous wink just before her helmet canopy turned opaque. Perl revved the accelerator and took off, burning out of the garage before Zed could get a hand on the bike.

"Leave," he managed to finish, watching as Perl sped into the night. She was already long gone. And he was as close to a system crash with anger and humiliation as he had ever been before.

"I am . . . a complete and utter and unforgivable IDIOT."

"**YES**," intoned Bit, flashing from polyhedron to square and back again.

Zed looked down and saw the antique widget floating with friendly-but-annoying bounciness at his feet.

"I am also completely screwed," Zed said aloud to the widget.

Before Bit could respond in the affirmative or negative, Zed kicked him across the garage as hard as he could.

* * *

Beck sighed deeply: *here we go again . . . AGAIN.*

The Coliseum's game floor had lost its novelty as Pavel led Beck and Cutler back to the center of the arena, their footfalls punctuated by an uproarious ovation from the crowd. Beck wondered if the spectators ever left. *No*, he thought, *not when there are more Games to be seen.*

Pavel raised his hands to the crowd, urging silence.

"Greetings, programs! Today is a momentous occasion. For not only do you share the privilege of seeing *two* highly skilled combatants battle for survival . . ."

Again, Beck thought.

"But now you can watch as merciful General Tesler allows them to compete for the greatest prize of all . . . FREEDOM!"

I'll believe it when I'm free, Beck thought.

"The winner of the next round will be RELEASED!" shouted Pavel, and the crowd cheered its approval.

It was almost too good to be true. And in Beck's experience, such things were empty promises to invariably be yanked away just before you could grasp that which you worked so hard to achieve.

Beck turned to Pavel. He may as well get on with it. All this back-and-forth—fight and escape, capture and fight again—was making him truly weary.

"Who are we fighting?" he said to the general's loyal toady.

Pavel grinned mischievously and snapped his fingers. Just then a beacon shined down from above, falling squarely on the shoulders of Beck and Cutler and framing them in a single all-revealing column of light. Beck and Cutler looked at one another. Cutler was confused. Beck wasn't. It all made perfect, terrible sense.

They gazed skyward as an even brighter spotlight blazed upon General Tesler's secure observation deck. Tesler was making his way to the deck's balcony, hushing the crowd, which applauded eagerly. They were simply going through the motions, acknowledging the great military leader as was accustomed. *Conditioned.* But what they were really here for was the Games. At Tesler's urging, the arena fell dead silent.

"*Who* are you fighting?" Tesler repeated.

Just say it already, Beck thought.

"Why, *EACH OTHER* of course."

Beck looked at Cutler. Cutler was stunned. Beck wasn't. Together, they had taken down a small squadron of seasoned soldiers-turned-gladiators, not to mention some of the best riders Beck had ever seen. Separate, they were Games fodder like any other doomed prisoners.

"To the death," Tesler added.

This time, the cheers were quite real.

CHAPTER 13

PAVEL BOWED THEATRICALLY and stepped off the gaming platform as it began to rise up, carrying Beck and Cutler into full view of the cheering, and carnage-hungry, crowd.

"How quickly they turn, huh? They expect us to fight each other?" said Beck.

Cutler smiled wanly. As an ISO—specifically an ISO who had fought in the war to eradicate all ISOs—he had less faith in the basic goodness of most programs.

"*Derez* each other," Cutler corrected. "That crowd won't be satisfied until one of us is in pieces."

"They can't make us do it. Not if we stand together."

Beck looked up at Tesler's booth—at Tesler himself—and stood facing the general with his arms folded defiantly.

The gesture was clear: *I'm not moving. I'm not fighting. No way.*

Cutler did the same. His solidarity with Beck was met with boos and catcalls from the crowd.

Tesler smiled and clapped his hands together just once. It wasn't approval, it was a *command*. Beck and Cutler watched as translucent light walls slid up all around the gaming platform, generated by hidden receptors sunk into the static tiling. The walls locked into place, edges merging in a crackle of energy. And then the walls began to move, encroaching on Beck and Cutler, starting to slowly close as a single diminishing cylinder. The general looked right at Beck as he spoke.

"When there's a winner, the walls stop."

Beck touched one of the walls. It thrummed with energy, but did not repulse him nor derez him. It didn't have to. It just kept pushing on Beck, moving inexorably toward the center of the gaming platform.

"If there's no winner, they don't stop."

Cutler joined Beck, digging in his heels as he pushed against the creeping wall, to no avail.

"Fight, or be crushed," said Tesler, and then the general turned and took a seat offered by Paige.

Beck stared up at the crowd. Clu's omnipresent image was beamed around the auditorium from various projectors. The leader's presence, albeit in holographic form, served as propaganda to all the programs, brainwashing them to his particular brand of malevolence. Fear kept the Grid in check.

"It can't end like this," said Beck.

But Beck knew he was running out of options. He reminded himself that Tron—*any* Tron for that matter, "next" or otherwise—would fight to the bitter end, or have a series of plans and counter-plans ready for even a no-win scenario such as this: *kill or be killed*.

Beck breathed deeply and resigned himself to not hesitating this time. He raised his identity disc and advanced on Cutler with a determined look. He had no other choice.

"Cutler, you've got to fight me."

"What?" said Cutler, backing up right into the advancing wall of light.

"One of us has to survive this. And it has to be you."

"What are you talking about, Beck? We can beat them!"

"No," said Beck. "Not this time."

Cutler shook his head, but Beck continued.

"Don't you see? If we *both* get derezzed, there will be no one left to continue the fight. They'll win. We can't let that happen. So attack me."

Beck lashed at Cutler with his disc. And as Beck had counted on, Cutler reflexively blocked the blow with his own disc. He was used to fighting and defending, and if push came to shove, he'd fight for his life. Beck just needed to keep on pushing and shoving.

"Are you crazy?!" Cutler shouted, sidestepping another strike. "This is *exactly* what they want!"

"Then let's give them what they want. Now come on!"

Beck threw a punch at Cutler's head. Cutler caught Beck's fist in his palm, holding it tightly and squeezing.

"No. I won't fight you."

Beck looked into Cutler's eyes and saw a panoply of emotions: anger. Betrayal. Sadness. For an ISO, one of the last of his kind, friends were a rare commodity on the Grid. He didn't want to fight. He *wouldn't* fight.

"Fine. Then you'll die a coward."

Beck shoved as hard as he could, then emphasized his words with a kick to Cutler's chest that sent the ISO sliding back along the ground and slamming hard against the slowly encroaching light wall. Cutler pushed himself up from the platform and locked eyes with Beck. He retrieved his identity disc from the back of his battlesuit and mouthed a few words that were barely audible over the roar of the crowd. But Beck knew what Cutler said as he came charging toward Beck.

"Tron lives. You said so."

Beck almost didn't raise his disc as Cutler came swinging. The bladed curves of their discs connected in a surge of sizzling energy. The crowd cheered. Cutler had rage in his eyes and swung again, more forceful this time. But it was fear, not desperation. Cutler's forward momentum flung him across the platform—what was remaining of the dwindling space—and into the curved wall of light.

Cutler got up and threw his disc with a grunt. Beck easily blocked the spinning disc, which caromed off the diminishing cylinder in which they found themselves. Cutler caught the disc in a spin, revolving around to hurl it back with even greater force. Beck blocked it again, this time sending

Cutler's disc skittering across the platform to land at his feet.

"Is that the *best* you got?" taunted Beck.

Cutler snorted and took off on a run in a curve around the shrinking platform space, an obvious attempt to draw out Beck. Beck didn't take the bait, instead heading in the opposite direction.

"Quit fooling around. You're not fooling anyone," said Beck.

Cutler responded by throwing his disc again, aiming for Beck's feet. Without breaking stride, Beck ran up the side of the wall and was momentarily perpendicular to the platform floor as Cutler's disc slid under him and missed its target. Beck propelled himself off the wall in a dramatic back-flip that elicited hoots and hollers from a large portion of the audience. As he landed, Beck fired off his disc, not at Cutler but at Cutler's disc. It struck with another sizzle of energy, sending the disc spinning away . . . and right into Cutler's waiting hand.

Beck retrieved his own disc as it ricocheted off the light wall, watching as Cutler momentarily lost his balance. Beck hesitated, but on purpose this time. It was enough time for Cutler to right himself and throw his disc harder than ever before. Beck deflected Cutler's disc as it zoomed right at his head, but the force of blocking the potential killshot knocked him down with sufficient impact to knock the breath out of him too. Beck wheezed, and then did his best to reassert his mock bravado.

"Much better," he said.

Cutler wasted no time, leaping to catch his disc and then landing right on top of Beck. The breath was knocked out of him again, and Beck found his arms pinned beneath Cutler's legs as he knelt upon him. Cutler raised his disc.

Beck felt a twinge of panic, but he had resigned himself to this fate. He knew what had to be done, which is why he goaded Cutler into this reluctant death match in the first place.

"I'm ready," he whispered.

Cutler brought his disc crashing down with all his might.

The disc imbedded in the platform surface just micrometers from Beck's head, barely missing him. The crowd let out a collective gasp. For Beck, it was worse than having the breath knocked out of him *twice*. It was as if all the air in the arena had been sucked out. Or maybe it was the force from Cutler's disc, as it first WHOOSHED, then WHACKED as it imbedded into the platform. Cutler left himself defenseless, standing with his disc still stuck in the platform. He stared up at the crowd, scanning the arena until he spied Tesler's booth. The general and the prisoner locked gazes. The crowd waited for someone to break the silence. Cutler was the first.

"I forfeit. He wins. Let him go."

Beck couldn't believe what he was hearing. *Cutler, I was giving you a chance. . . .*

He got to his feet and stood inches from Cutler, his back to Tesler as the programs conversed in hushed tones.

"What are you *doing*?" Beck managed through gritted teeth. He was angry, and he didn't want Tesler or the audience to hear them. Not that it was possible now with the crowd's divided opinions on Cutler's forfeiture. Half the audience booed him. The other half applauded Cutler's unexpected sacrifice. Maybe there was hope for the denizens of Argon City, after all. . . .

In General Tesler's observation booth, Tesler turned to Pavel with a perplexed look that neither Pavel or Paige had seen before.

"Did he say he *forfeits*?"

"Yes, sir," stammered Pavel.

Things weren't exactly going according to Pavel's plan, and Paige marveled at how the worm had turned for the bootlicking aide.

"He can't do that," said Tesler, though it sounded more like a query than a statement.

"I think he just did, sir," said Pavel, already regretting his words.

Luckily for Pavel, the General turned back to look down on the platform and the two vexing problems who just wouldn't lie down and derez like other doomed prisoners.

Below, Cutler faced Beck. Cutler's expression was stony. Resolute. There was no turning back for him.

"You're the better fighter, Beck. If we want to defeat Clu, you're the right program to do it."

Beck shook his head.

"I don't know if you're being noble . . . or if you're just plain *crazy*," he said.

Cutler smiled. "Tron lives," he said.

"I'm not so sure of that," said Beck.

"I am," replied Cutler without hesitation.

Tesler was fuming now. He briefly thought Beck and Cutler had turned on each other, but that clearly wasn't the case. No matter. Tesler knew what the final outcome was going to be: both programs broken and derezzed.

"If they both wish to be derezzed, I have no problem obliging them," Tesler hissed.

The audience, however, had different feelings. The rising chorus of boos had morphed into a chant that echoed throughout the tesseract.

"ONE GOES FREE! ONE GOES FREE!"

Paige took particular note of the crowd's general attitude toward Tesler's edict. *Rules are rules* . . .

"Sir, they might have a problem if you do that," said Paige.

She had become more outspoken again as Pavel slunk away, the toady trying very hard to become invisible as the crowd thundered inside the gaming arena.

"You did promise the crowd freedom," she said.

"So?"

Paige spoke plainly. The general listened. He had once spared her life in order to mold her to his specifications. Therefore, he had a certain respect for her assessment, since it was largely a reflection of what he might do if he was unencumbered by rank or status or having the responsibility of never failing Clu.

"So you've got an image to uphold as the benevolent leader. One should go free. But the other . . ." Paige looked right at Beck.

Tesler looked at the crowd, a rising tide of that threatened to turn ugly. The Coliseum was unfinished. The first rule of a riot is that anything not nailed down is apt to be picked up and thrown. Tesler certainly didn't want to report to Almighty Clu that the Grid's greatest attraction in the Sea of Simulation was torn asunder by rebellious programs because Tesler didn't keep a promise he had made in full view of the masses.

He sighed. They were supposed to be *his* crowd. . . .

"Very well," he said with great reluctance.

On the gaming platform, Beck and Cutler stood their ground as the light walls crept within inches of crushing them utterly.

"Nice knowing—" Beck didn't even have a chance to finish his good-bye.

The walls began to retract, retreating much faster than they had been advancing. From above, General Tesler's voice boomed over the many floating speaker widgets that worked in concert to make sure the general's voice never fell on deaf ears.

"PROGRAMS OF ARGON!"

The audience silenced in less than a heartbeat.

"Both of these enemies deserve to perish. But we are not savages. We are civilized programs. I made a promise to you, and I intend to uphold it."

The crowd showed their approval with a fusillade of applause. Tesler waited for the clapping to subside and then pointed at Beck as he stood on the gaming platform.

"Number five, you will be rewarded your freedom . . . even though you clearly failed to earn it."

Beck swallowed hard. This was not what he had planned. Tesler waited for the gravity of the judgment to sink in before addressing Cutler with unmasked contempt.

"As for number three . . . at the end of the next cycle, you will meet your end at Argon Square. A public execution by way of particle disintegration, where you will be derezzed, bit by excruciating bit."

Cutler stood unwavering, unafraid. The crowd cheered its approval. Each dissenting half got what it wanted. Freedom and death, six of one and a half dozen of the other. Tesler basked in the mass adulation. "No program makes a mockery of the Games and lives."

Tesler turned to Paige and Pavel, who was slinking near the exit.

"Now that's what I call win-win," said the general.

Little did Tesler know that he was, in a reality to be made apparent soon enough, just half right.

CHAPTER 14

FOLLOWING GENERAL TESLER'S SENTENCING, the audience dispersed quickly. The crowd came to the Games for violence, and they had it in their grasp. A pair of Sentries swooped in to lead Beck out of the arena. More Sentries took custody of Cutler and were in the process of remanding him to a holding cell. He looked back at his former teammate.

"Beck!" Cutler broke free from the Sentries, taking off toward his friend. "Promise me," he called. "Don't stop fighting!"

The Sentries tackled Cutler, with more arriving in short order to help restrain him. It was a disproportionate show of force, and in the scuffle Cutler's ISO badge was torn from his arm. The badge fell to the floor, its light band retracting back into its stylized circle, the sigil inert. It was a bad omen. The Sentries didn't notice the badge as they rushed to bind Cutler.

"Promise me you'll find Tron and *join* him," Cutler managed, even as the Sentries were dragging him away.

"Promise—" Cutler tried to shout, but a Sentry punched him in the jaw, silencing him.

Beck lunged for Cutler's lost ISO badge, his hand closing over it just as the Sentries hauled him away . . . *to freedom.* . . .

Fifteen minutes later, Beck raced toward the mountains on his Light Cycle, his baton returned only after Beck was stripped out of the number-five battlesuit he had worn to some small acclaim in his brief second career as a reluctant gladiator. Beck donned his mechanic's togs once more. As he rode, Beck doubled back upon his trail several times and even waited behind parts of the landscape to see if he was being followed. He wouldn't put it past Tesler or his flunkies. Beck ran diagnostics on both his suit and cycle to make sure neither was bugged. Everything checked out clean, so he continued on his way through the Outlands to Tron's lair.

Safe within the shielded confines of his hideout, Tron

himself listened as Beck related the experiences at the Coliseum in exacting detail. Beck talked without interruption, holding Cutler's ISO badge in his hands the entire time. Beck sat in darkness. Tron was somewhere in the lair, but out of Beck's sight.

"We had a choice. Me or Cutler. I'm not sure we chose the *right* one." Beck toggled the ISO badge to life and regarded the illuminated sigil. "He's the real hero. He could've made a *difference*," Beck continued.

"You managed to survive the Games and walk away with all your limbs intact. Seems like you did okay," said Tron, his voice echoing strangely to Beck.

"I let them take Cutler away to be derezzed. I failed. *Again*."

The lights came up and Beck was surprised as a medical bed lowered down from an strange tank in the ceiling. Beck was more stunned to see Tron suspended in a pool of glowing liquid—some sort of nutrient bath or restorative—and looking in pretty bad shape. Tron grasped the lip of the tank and lifted himself out of the pool, the energized liquid viscous and goopy as it dripped off him. He moved slowly. *Still not at 100-percent capacity*, Beck noted. Not that Beck wasn't stiff and sore from his marathon combat excursions at the Coliseum.

"Are you all right?" Beck said.

Tron smiled, laughing a little.

"Jumping over canyons takes its toll on my injuries. I'll be fine. And you have more pressing matters to worry about. Your friend—he's still alive, right?"

"Yeah. Until next cycle that is."

"Then you haven't failed . . . *yet*."

From his seat, Beck looked up at Tron. Even broken down and convalescing, he still inspired hope.

"Tron lives," said Beck, closing his hand around Cutler's badge, the sigil warm in his palm.

"Of course he does," said Tron.

CHAPTER 15

IT WAS STILL NIGHT WHEN BECK rolled up to Able's Garage. He had made the trip back to Argon City from Tron's secret lair in record time, but still took the time to slow down and avoid any Sentries or Recognizers on patrol. Though he had 'earned' his freedom from Tesler, Beck had suspicions that even the most minor infraction would send him right back to the arena—with no reprieve this time.

Beck entered the garage as quietly as possible so as not to disturb a sleeping Able in the upstairs living quarters. He went right to his locker and prepared to carry out his admittedly crazy plan to save Cutler.

Beck was outside the garage and about to mount his Light Cycle when Zed came running after him, desperate to stop him.

"Beck!"

Beck paused as Zed struggled to catch his breath and speak at the same time.

"I'm glad I found you. Look, I did something really stupid and I could really use your help—"

Beck rolled his eyes. Zed couldn't have picked a worse time. Whatever it was, Zed's problem would have to wait. Cutler's time was short, and he was Beck's *only* priority at the moment. "I'm sorry, Zed. I gotta go. Did you ask Mara? Maybe she can help."

Without another word, Beck toggled his Light Cycle and roared off. Zed watched his friend go. Then he took a deep breath and went back into the garage.

A few blocks from Able's Garage, Beck pulled into a dimly illuminated alley and ducked behind a Dumpster, a quiet corner where he wouldn't be seen from the street. Beck attached his "renegade" device to his back. Instantly, his mechanic's uniform reconfigured into the renegade's costume.

Beck's Light Cycle changed as well. It took on a fiercer silhouette, and both rider and machine were ready for action.

* * *

Back at the garage, Mara busied herself retrofitting a plasma cannon on a Light Tank. Zed walked into the repair bay, silently freaking out. Mara watched him curiously. Zed was so absorbed in his personal crisis that, for once, he didn't notice or acknowledge Mara. She chalked it up to a crush. Perhaps pretty Perl had left her imprint on Zed.

"I can't believe I let her . . ." muttered Zed.

"Zed?" said Mara.

"Maybe there's a way to fix this . . ."

"Zed?"

"Oh, who am I kidding? I'm FINISHED!"

"ZED!"

He stopped and looked up at Mara.

"What's wrong with you?" she said.

"Me? Nothing. Everything. It's been great working with you, Mara. I'm sure we'll still meet up here and there. I'm going to miss this place. Maybe Able will let me visit sometime."

Mara put down her tools and set aside work on the plasma cannon. She was genuinely concerned now. Zed was a pain in the neck sometimes, but he was still her friend.

"Zed. Calm down. Now, what happened?"

Zed sat down and took a deep breath.

"Okay, so remember Perl, the girl from the club? Big mistake. I kinda brought her back here to the garage and, well . . ." Mara's eyes went wide with anger as Zed told her what happened.

Mara took a deep breath before plopping down next to Zed. Before she could speak, Able walked into the repair bay. He seemed bothered by something other than his usual complaints: Clu. Beck. How things were better in the 'old days.' Beck. Patrons with no appreciation for his work. Beck . . .

"Zed?" said Able.

Zed stared at the floor of the garage.

"Have you seen my baton?" Able said as he searched through the racks of tools and parts.

Zed's panic was evident to Mara, but not their boss.

"Which baton? You've got a million batons."

Able chortled, clapping Zed on the back as he continued his futile search for a baton that had not been in the garage since Perl absconded with it hours before.

"The baton. My favorite Light Cycle. You know"—Able leaned

close, laying a hand alongside his mouth and whispering—"the one that belonged to *Flynn*."

Zed tried not to look guilty, which only served to make him look as guilty as he could be. Mara watched him edge closer to the verge of spontaneously derezzing, and she let him dangle there just a bit more.

"Funny story about that," said Zed. "You should sit down. You see, I—"

Mara looked right at Zed. He didn't . . .

"Oh, I totally forgot! We're late!" she said, taking Zed's arm, dragging him to standing.

"The thing. You know. *The. Thing.*"

Mara led Zed away from Able's search, out of the repair bay, out of the garage, and out of a heap of trouble . . . for now.

"What are you doing?" said Zed, breaking away to face Mara.

"I am helping you get that bike back from Perl."

"Wow, that obviously . . . I mean . . . we'll never find her."

"Maybe not. And maybe Able will take you apart for spare parts to build a scale-model replica of Flynn's actual bike. Which we can find."

"How? By hitting every club in Argon and looking for all the dejected, humiliated programs left in her wake?"

Mara held up a small device, a digital compass with a blinking red node marking the movement of an object tied to its electronic imprint. It was a tracker.

"Come on," said Mara, following the compass's orientation, letting the red node lead her.

Zed watched her for a moment and then followed. It looked like Mara was getting him out of trouble. *Again*.

Across the city, another recovery was in the offing. Clad in his renegade armor, Beck stood atop the monolithic I/O Tower high above Argon and waited as a convoy of Recognizers approached. Aboard one of the machines, awaiting his ignominious end, was Cutler. Beck was going to save his new friend, or die trying. Beck watched and waited, counting the Recognizers until he found the one he sought.

Stealthily, Beck pushed off from the tower and landed in a crouch on top of the head of the Recognizer. The vehicle canted just barely, not enough to warrant a pause in its flight plan as part of the convoy. Neither the Recognizer ahead nor the one behind reacted. Beck was undetected so far. Certain that no Sentries would be spilling out to arrest him, Beck opened a small relay hatch and jumped in.

A pair of guards looked up in surprise as the renegade descended upon them with ruthless speed and accuracy. Beck scissor-kicked one of them in the head as he jumped down from an access shaft. The guard was knocked out before he hit the floor.

The second guard lasted just a bit longer, regaining his wits to grab an electrified halberd from a wall panel.

"You shouldn't play with pointy objects, you know," said the renegade.

Behind the renegade's helmet, Beck felt momentarily discombobulated, such was the sensation of hearing his own voice modulated several octaves lower and laced with an electronic chaff that unnerved those in close proximity. *He was the renegade, after all . . .*

The guard lunged, electricity coruscating around the blade of the halberd. Beck took it from the guard, disarming him with ease and twirling the halberd around to smash him in the face with the weapon's blunt end.

"Toldja," said the renegade in a voice that sounded like the snarl of an engine.

Beck stepped over the bodies of the unconscious guards and made his way to the prison pods. He found Cutler inside a small cell, locked behind light bars. Cutler looked up, perhaps expecting his final meal before the public execution scheduled just hours hence.

His jaw dropped.

"Tron? Is it really you?"

Beck momentarily forgot that he was wearing his renegade suit, that his visor covered a face Cutler would have instantly recognized.

"Yeah, I'm—"

Even with the renegade suit's voice modulator, Beck swallowed hard and attempted to deepen his voice further. For the full effect . . .

"I'm Tron."

The renegade unsheathed his identity disc and pulverized the cell's control pad with a single quick slash. The light bars retracted instantly, powering down. Cutler's eyes were bright with hope. The renegade spoke in his deepest, most heroic voice: "Now let's get you out of here."

Beck knew it would be hard to finish the escape, but he also knew he would never give up. He had responsibilities greater than he could have imagined, but he was not alone. With the help of the original Tron and other brave programs, they could fight against Tesler and his army. They could fight against Clu. They could make the Grid free once more. And it was all going to start right here. He took a deep breath and turned to Cutler. "Let's go."